A Blue's Clues Chanukah

by Jessica Lissy
illustrated by Dan Kanemoto and Jennifer Oxley

Simon Spotlight/Nick Jr.
New York   London   Toronto   Sydney   Singapore

Note to Parents from Creators:
It's a *Blue's Clues* Chanukah party, and you and your child are invited! Join Blue and her friends as they celebrate family togetherness and explore traditional holiday activities like playing dreidel, cooking and eating special foods, lighting the menorah, and singing songs. *A Blue's Clues Chanukah* will introduce some of the concepts and customs of Chanukah while giving you and your child ideas about the many ways your family can enjoy the holiday together. For those who celebrate Chanukah and for those who are curious about it, it's a chance to learn and play!

For my parents, Maggie and David, and for my siblings, Micah and Rachel,
with admiration and with love for all the light you bring to my life–J. L.

Based on the TV series *Blue's Clues*® created by Traci Paige Johnson,
Todd Kessler, and Angela C. Santomero as seen on Nick Jr.®
On *Blue's Clues*, Joe is played by Donovan Patton. Photos by Joan Marcus.

SIMON SPOTLIGHT
An imprint of Simon & Schuster Children's Publishing Division
1230 Avenue of the Americas, New York, NY 10020
Copyright © 2003 Viacom International Inc.
Manufactured in the United States of America
First Edition   10 9 8 7 6 5 4 3 2 1
ISBN 0-689-85840-X

"Come quick, Blue!" said Joe. "The mail's here, and we got a letter!" Blue opened it up as fast as she could. It was an invitation to a Chanukah party from Orange Kitten! "I've never been to a Chanukah party before," said Blue.

"Me neither," said Joe.

Everyone got bundled up for the walk to Orange Kitten's house.

"What do you think we'll do at the party?" asked Joe.

"I think we'll see all of our friends," said Slippery.

"I think we'll help Orange Kitten celebrate Chanukah," said Tickety.

Just then Paprika spotted Orange Kitten's house.
"We're almost there!" she said.

"Happy Chanukah!" Orange Kitten greeted them. "We're cutting out decorations and making menorahs. Want to help?"

"Sure!" said Joe. "But what's a menorah?"

"A menorah is a special candle holder we use on Chanukah," explained Orange Kitten. "It has room for nine candles: That's one for each of the eight nights of Chanukah, plus a helper candle called the shammash to light all the others."

"Psst, Blue!" whispered Purple Kangaroo. "I'm not sure how to finish this menorah. How many more candle holders does it need?"

Blue counted carefully. "Three," she said, "and I'll help you make them!"

"Thanks!" said Purple Kangaroo.

When the menorahs were finished, Orange Kitten put them in the window.

"When people see our menorahs they'll remember that a miracle happened a long time ago," she said. "Some oil that was only supposed to burn one day lasted for eight whole days."

"Is that why Chanukah is eight days long?" asked Blue.

"Exactly!" said Orange Kitten.

"Tonight is the sixth night of Chanukah," said Orange Kitten, "so we need to put six candles in each of our menorahs."

"Mmm, what smells so good?" asked Joe.

"Latkes!" said Orange Kitten as she led everyone to the kitchen. "Latkes are potato pancakes, and they're my favorite Chanukah food."

"Are we doing a good job with your latke recipe, Orange Kitten?" asked Mr. Salt.

"Yup!" said Orange Kitten. "I can't wait to eat them."

Potatoes

Onion

Eggs

Salt

Oil

Blue peeked out the window. The sun had set and it was getting dark.

"Come on, everybody! It's time to light the Chanukah candles!" Orange Kitten called.

Everyone crowded around the window and watched as Orange Kitten sang some special blessings, and Mr. Salt and Mrs. Pepper carefully lit the candles in each menorah.

"The candles are all lit," said Orange Kitten. "That means it's time for . . ."

"... opening presents!" Everybody loved their gifts, especially the chocolate Chanukah gelt.

"Money you can eat—how wonderful!" said Mr. Salt.

"I'm glad you like it," said Orange Kitten. But Joe was confused.

"Um, Orange Kitten? What is this?" asked Joe.

"It's a dreidel," Orange Kitten explained. "It has Hebrew letters on it—Nun, Gimel, Hey, and Shin."

"Wow, thanks," said Joe. "It'll make a nice head-scratcher, or a clay-scraper, or a very small umbrella. . . ."

"Silly Joe!" said Orange Kitten. "Dreidel is a game you play with friends. Come and see!"

"You first, Periwinkle," said Orange Kitten. "Spin the dreidel and see which Hebrew letter lands facing up."

Periwinkle spun the dreidel—it landed on Shin.

"That means put one piece of Chanukah gelt in the pot," said Orange Kitten.

Magenta's dreidel landed on Hey. "Good spin, Magenta!" said
Orange Kitten. "You get half the pot!"

"Yay for Hey!" Magenta said as she took three pieces of gelt.
"Chocolate is my favorite!"

The latkes were ready! Everybody rushed to try them. "This is the first latke I've ever eaten," said Joe. "It's delicious!"

"They are even better with applesauce," suggested Orange Kitten.

"Do you want to hear my favorite Chanukah songs?" asked Orange Kitten.

"Absolutely!" said Joe. "We love to learn new songs."

"Great!" said Orange Kitten. "Let's sing!"

"Look," said Paprika. "Cinnamon is asleep."

"Yes," said Mr. Salt, "it's past his bedtime."

"It's past my bedtime, too, but I'm wide awake!" Paprika said proudly, trying not to yawn.

Chanukah, Oh Chanukah

Chanukah,
Oh Chanukah,
Come light the
menorah.
Let's have a party.
We'll all dance
the hora!

Little Dreidel

I have a little dreidel.
I made it out of clay.
And when it's dry and ready
Oh Dreidel I shall play.

"It's time to go home," said Mrs. Pepper, "but what a wonderful party that was, Orange Kitten!"

"Thank you! Happy Chanukah!" shouted Blue and all of her friends as they headed out into the cold.

"Happy Chanukah!" Orange Kitten called back. "See you at my Chanukah party next year!"